W9-BRT-630

Once, there was a gentleman whose wife died after a prolonged illness. He had a beautiful and sweet-natured daughter named Cinderella. The man married again, but his second wife turned out to be a cruel and haughty woman. Cinderella's stepmother had two daughters from her earlier marriage.

Cinderella's stepmother was rude to her and made her do all the household chores. Cinderella was treated harshly by her stepsisters also. Cinderella did all that she could to please them, but they bullied her and never thanked her for all that she did for them.

2

One day, a messenger arrived with an invitation to a royal ball from the Prince Charming. Cinderella's stepmother told her daughters excitedly, "It will be a grand ball, my dears. You must wear your finest dresses."
Cinderella's stepsisters were very excited and started preparing for the ball.

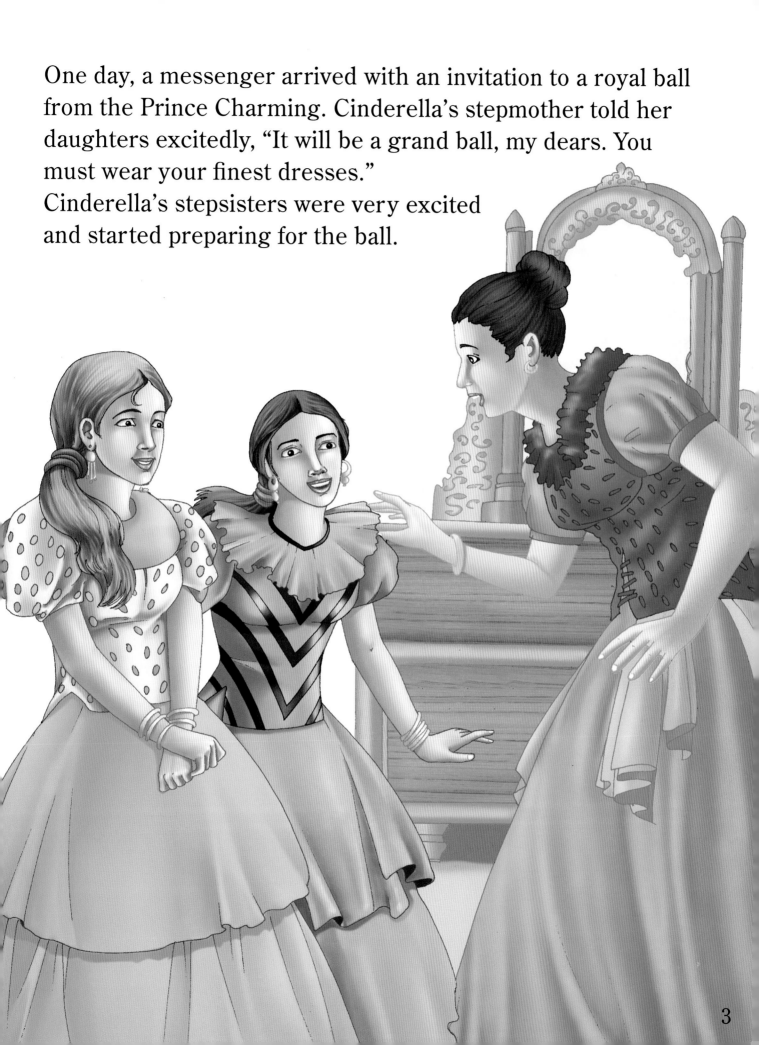

Cinderella too wished to attend the ball. "Am I invited too? What will I wear?" asked Cinderella. "You will never be invited to a royal ball. Just look at yourself," said her stepmother. The finest silks were purchased from which Cinderella was asked to make ball gowns. She worked from morning till night and soon the beautiful gowns were ready.

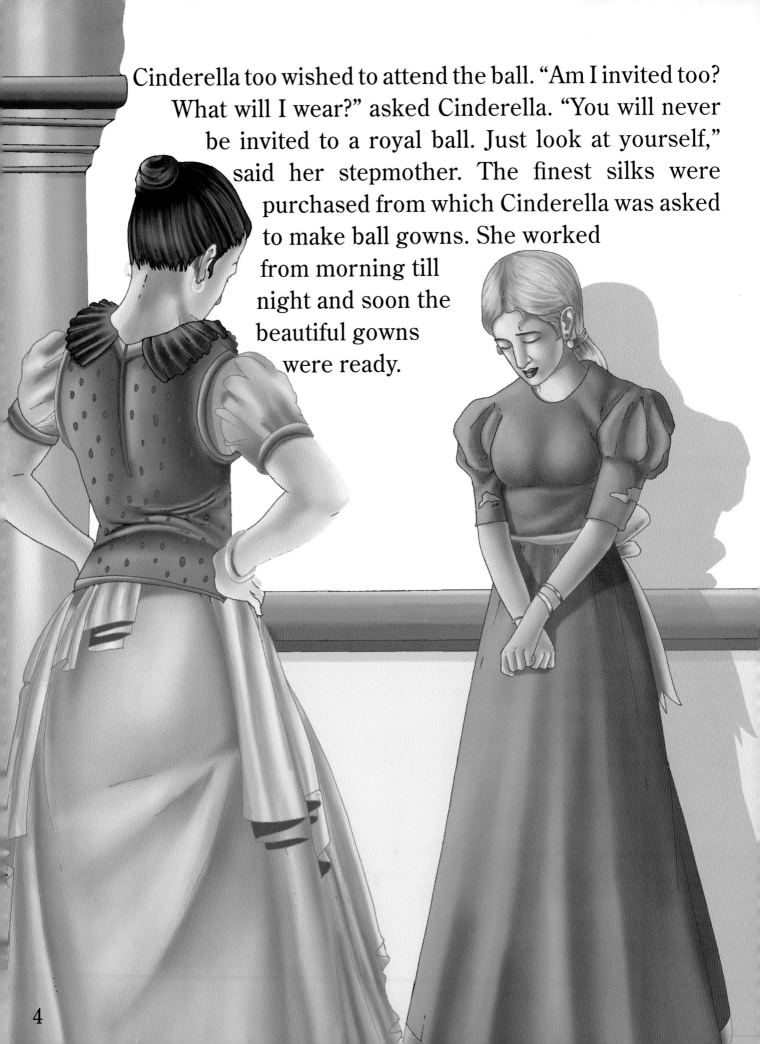

At last, the day of the ball arrived. Cinderella's stepmother and stepsisters left for the ball dressed magnificently. When she saw them leave, Cinderella sighed, "I wish I could go to the ball too."

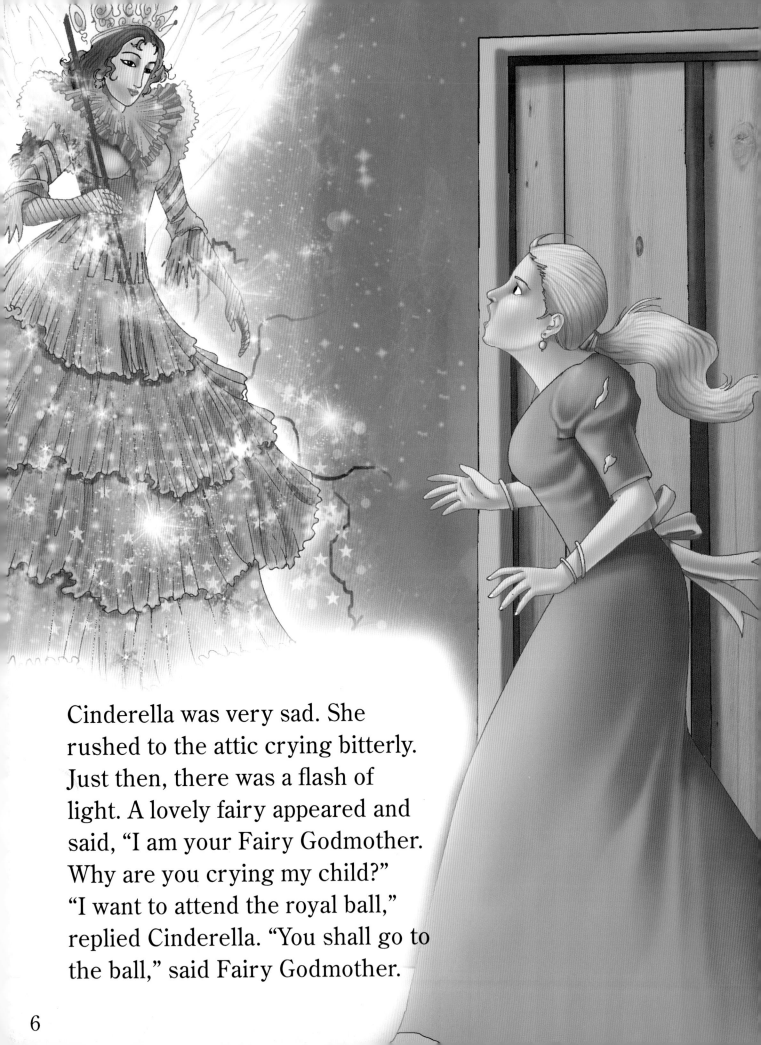

Cinderella was very sad. She rushed to the attic crying bitterly. Just then, there was a flash of light. A lovely fairy appeared and said, "I am your Fairy Godmother. Why are you crying my child?" "I want to attend the royal ball," replied Cinderella. "You shall go to the ball," said Fairy Godmother.

"But how? Look at me and my clothes," said Cinderella. "Get up dear and do as I say," continued Fairy Godmother. "Fetch me a pumpkin from the garden and four mice that you will find in the trap. Also, get me a frog from the garden pond." Cinderella rushed to the garden and returned with a pumpkin, four mice and a frog.

Fairy Godmother touched them with her magic wand. The pumpkin became a shining coach, the mice became four fine horses and the frog changed into a coachman. Cinderella was pleasantly surprised to see all this.

Next, Fairy Godmother touched Cinderella with her wand and changed her old, torn clothes into the most beautiful gown that Cinderella had ever seen. Then, she gave Cinderella a pair of the prettiest glass slippers. "Well, my child, now you are ready to go to the ball," said she.

As Cinderella sat in the carriage, Fairy Godmother cautioned her, "Child, now you may leave for the ball, but remember to leave the ball before midnight, for then, my magic will run out." Cinderella promised that she would return before midnight. She thanked Fairy Godmother and left for the ball.

When Cinderella entered the ballroom, everyone was mesmerized by her beauty. Even her stepmother and stepsisters were unable to recognise her. Prince Charming fell in love with her when he saw her and danced only with her. She happily danced with the Prince, but forgot about her promise to Fairy Godmother. Time sped by and then the clock began to strike twelve.

When Cinderella heard the clock strike twelve, she rushed out from the ballroom. As Cinderella ran down the stairway, one of her glass slippers fell off her feet. She didn't stop but hurried away in her carriage. The Prince stood there speechless, holding her glass slipper in his hand.

By the time Cinderella reached home, her dress had changed back to rags and the carriage was gone. When her stepsisters returned with their mother, Cinderella asked "How was the ball?" "It was simply magnificent but the Prince danced only with a very beautiful Princess," replied her stepsisters.

Meanwhile, the Prince wanted to find the beautiful girl who had fled from the ball, as he had fallen madly in love with her. But no one could tell anything about her. Then the Prince thought of a solution. A proclamation was made that the Prince would marry the girl whose foot would fit into the glass slipper. Soon, a minister was sent around the kingdom with the glass slipper.

At last, the Minister came to Cinderella's house. The stepsisters tried really hard to squeeze their feet into the slipper, but they could not. Then the Minister noticed the shy Cinderella standing in one corner. He asked her to try the glass slipper on. Her stepsisters laughed aloud as the Minister beckoned Cinderella to try the slipper.

The stepsisters suddenly stopped laughing when the Minister exclaimed, "The slipper fits her!" Everybody was surprised! Just then, Cinderella took out the other glass slipper from her pocket, which was a perfect match to the one brought by the Minister. The very next day, Cinderella was married to the Prince and they lived happily ever after.